THE
MAGPIE

TO BARBARA.
WISH YOU COULD
HAVE READ THIS.

TO KIM.
YOU DON'T HAVE
TO READ THIS.

TO WHAT I OWE THIS DO TRIBUTE?
SPEAK WITCH. WHAT IS IT YOU WANT?
I...UM...

YES, I DO NOT UNDERSTAND.
BUT IF YOU WANT HIM, TAKE HIM. I WILL NEVER FIND WHAT HE SEEKS.
I DO NOT WANT WORTHLESS SACRIFICE ANYMORE.

AMANDA?

SORRY, TEACHER SAID YOU COULD CATCH ME UP ON WORK.

HUH?

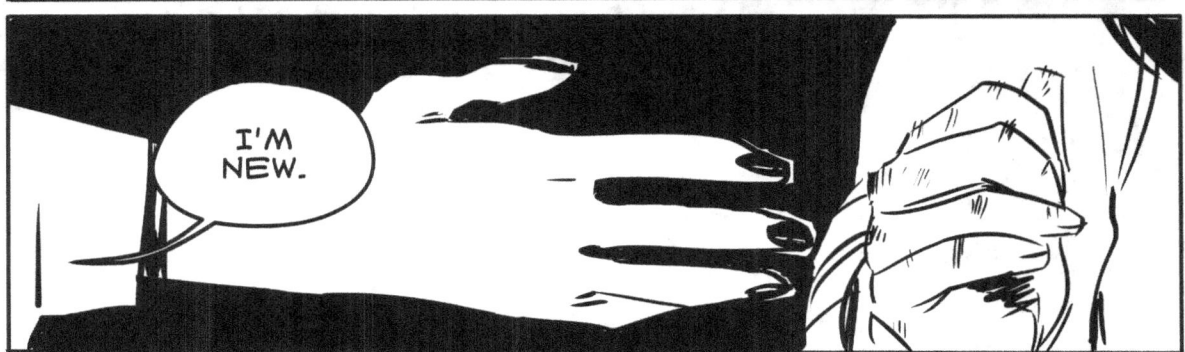

CAN I SHARE YOUR COPY OF THE BOOK?

APARENLTY THIS SCHOOL IS SEVERELY UNDERFUNDED OR SOMETHING.

I'M SURE GRANNY'S GOT A COPY LAYING AROUND SOMEWHERE. I THINK SHE TOOK LIT COURSES AT SOME POINT–

HOW DID YOU GET HERE?

SCHOOL? I WALKED?

NO, HOW DID YOU MOVE IN?

DROVE?

NEVER MIND.

DON'T LISTEN TO AMANDA, SHE'S A FREAK.

WE'LL SHARE OUR BOOKS, DON'T WORRY ABOUT IT.

WHAT TOOK YOU SO LONG, PICKLE?

DID YOU SERIOUSLY FORGET YOUR COAT AGAIN?

COME ON WE'LL GRAB SOMETHING FROM THE LOST AND FOUND.

HOW'S THE FOOT?

IT HURTS...

YOUR DAD'S STILL NOT TAKING YOU TO A DOCTOR?

LOST AND FOUND

YOU TELL YOUR DAD THAT, IF YOU DON'T GET TO THE DOCTOR,

I'LL BEAT HIM UP.

HEY AMANDA!

HUH? I THOUGHT YOU WERE GETTING THE TOUR.

NAH, I HAD TO LEAVE EARLY. I PROMISED MY GRANDMA I'D CLEAR THE WALKWAY.

IS IT ALWAYS BLIZZARDING HERE? OR AM I JUST LUCKY?

ALWAYS.

LAME.

SO, YOU'RE A BIT OF A BLACK SHEEP IN TOWN?

YEP.

THAT THE KID YOU'RE BABYSITTING?

YEP.

OKAY, HONESTY HOUR, I WAS TALKING TO TAMMY AND SHE SAYS YOU'RE A BITCH AND A DYKE.

GREAT.

YEAH, AND BITCH, WHATEVER. I GET THAT, YOU'RE PRETTY SOUR. BUT I BAILED ON THE DYKE THING.

I DON'T CARE, SO...

GRANDMA?

SURE, LIE TO YOURSELF,

NO SKIN OFF MY NOSE.

IT'S FINE.

I MEAN IT'S NOT FINE AT ALL. WE WERE KIND OF SHORT ON CASH... SHE DIDN'T EVEN LEAVE A NOTE.

SORRY...

YOU SHOULDN'T TELL ANYONE ABOUT THAT. PEOPLE HERE GET REALLY CRUEL.

CHRIS?
YOU CRYING?

YOU OKAY?

SHE'S ACTING OUT AGAIN. AMANDA'S BABYSITTING DYLAN TONIGHT, BUT I DON'T KNOW WHAT TO DO.

SHE HATES HIM.

I COULD TALK TO HER.

YEAH, BUT *OW*...

NO SYMPATHY.

TRIXIE, HANNAH SAID SHE'D STOP BY TO PICK YOU UP. IT'S SO NICE TO HAVE YOU OVER.

IT'S BEEN MY PLEASURE. YOU HAVE A BEAUTIFUL HOUSE.

THANKS, TRIXIE.

AMANDA, I HOPE CHRIS DOESN'T THINK THAT DYLAN'S STAYING THE NIGHT. I NEED HIM OUT BEFORE BOOK CLUB.

WHAT'S WITH THAT?

THAT'S RULE TWO. DYLAN IS AN ANOMALY.

AN ANOMALY?

WAIT, ARE YOU COMING?

DOWN THE DRIVEWAY, THEN I'M GOING HOME.

OH, OKAY...

BUT YEAH, NO ONE LIKES DYLAN.

IT'S A RULE.

PICKLE'S A BITER.

NO KIDDING.

IS THAT WHY PEOPLE HATE HIM?

NOPE, HE'S AN AVERY. NOBODY LIKES THE AVERYS, IT'S BEST NOT TO INTERACT WITH THEM IF YOU CAN AVOID IT.

AND YOU BABYSIT FOR THEM?

YES, AND I'M *SO* POPULAR.

TRIX LEFT THEN, DID SHE?

I THINK SO...

SHE AND AMANDA ARE GETTING ALONG LIKE FISH AND WATER.

THAT'S A SHOCK.

TAMMY GAVE HER THE GRAND TOUR. SHE'S SO MUCH MORE LIVELY THAN AMANDA –

NOT THAT SHE ISN'T LOVELY, MARGIE.

THANK YOU...

SO, HANNAH, HOW'S TRIXIE TAKING THE MOVE?

AS WELL AS SHE CAN BE, GIVEN THE CIRCUMSTANCES...

THE MOVE'S BEEN GREAT... BUT I DON'T KNOW HOW SHE'LL RECOVER.

I DIDN'T KNOW BERNIE HAD A CHILD.

BUT THERE SHE WAS, CAUGHT IN THAT MESS.

I DON'T UNDERSTAND PEOPLE....

HOW ARE YOU TAKING THINGS?

ITS ODD. SHE'S BEEN GONE SO LONG, IT'S ALMOST NICE TO HAVE THE CLOSURE.

PLEASE, DON'T MAKE THIS ABOUT ME.

DENIS?

I TOLD YOU BOOK CLUB IS TONIGHT.

YEAH...

WELL?

YOU WANTED MORE TIME WITH ME, RIGHT?

I DID. BUT YOU KNEW I'D BE BUSY NOW.

YOU KNEW.

YOU'RE NOT GOING OUTSIDE, ARE YOU?

I DON'T HAVE A CHOICE.

YOU'RE RIGHT. *YOU'RE BLIND,* THERE IS NO WAY YOU ARE GOING OUT IN THIS WEATHER.

MARGIE, THIS IS SERIOUS.

LOOK WHO CAME HOME EARLY.

HELLO DENIS, I FORGOT MARGIE EVEN HAD A HUSBAND.

I KNOW, SO ELUSIVE.

NOW, I DON'T WANT TO SOUND LIKE A SNOOP... BUT YOU WEREN'T TALKING ABOUT THE AVERYS THERE?

SORRY, THEY'RE ON MY MIND IS ALL.

IS THIS ABOUT THAT BRAT?

NO... BUT DO TELL.

WELL, MY SUSAN WAS PLAYING NICELY WHEN HE ATTACKS HER. UNPROVOKED.

SHE STILL HAS THE BITE MARKS.

THAT CHILD. I KNOW KIDS ARE HELL, BUT I THINK IT NEEDS A NICE PADDED ROOM WITH THE REST OF THEM.

AGREED.

PSYCHOPATH.

DENIS, *SIT.*

AMANDA?

WHAT...?

DYLAN?

Sixteen-Year-Old Bernadette Gille Missing

BAM

AMANDA?

IS THIS YOUR PLACE?

SLAM

DYLAN, WHAT HAPPENED?

MOTHER'S MAD.

MORNING, LOCKER BUDDY.

SO, HOW WAS THE WALK?

FREEZING AND I PASSED OUT.

THAT'S NOT THE WORST PART.

I WOKE UP IN THE AVERY'S HOUSE...

IT WAS WEIRD.

THERE WASN'T ANY INSULATION,

CROWS...

AND BLOOD.

BLOOD? WHOSE BLOOD?

DYLAN'S? I DIDN'T STAY LONG TO ASK.

OH GOD, WE NEED TO CALL THE POLICE OR SOMETHING.

LEAN TOWARDS "OR SOMETHING," THE POLICE DON'T MAKE IT OUT HERE.

NOT IN THIS WEATHER.

COME ON, I NEED TO THINK THIS OUT MORE...

THERE WERE ALL THESE NEWSPAPERS ABOUT MISSING PEOPLE.

IT'S DUMB.... BUT MAYBE SOME PEOPLE DO ESCAPE.

THAT'S NOT DUMB AT ALL.

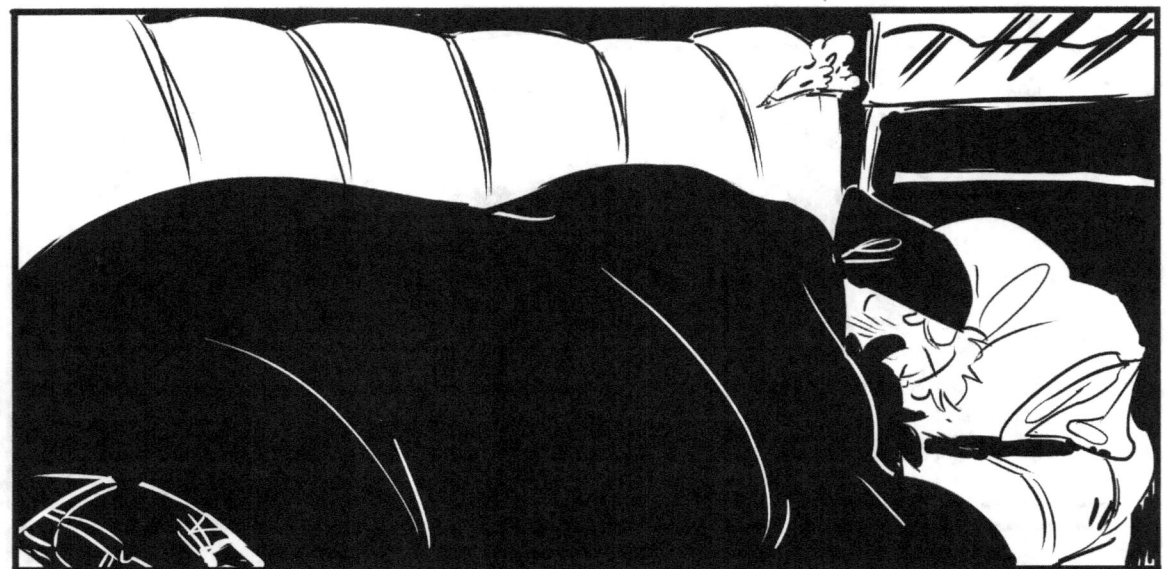

MADE IT THROUGH ANOTHER NIGHT...

YOU'LL CATCH YOUR DEATH AVOIDING US LIKE THAT.

SORRY... I GOT WRAPPED UP IN THINGS....

FINCH... WERE YOU THE ONE THAT TOOK AMANDA IN?

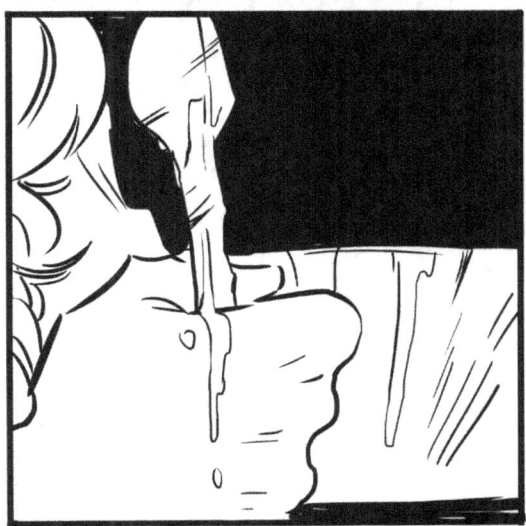

BERNADETTE?

Sixteen-Year-Old Bernadette Gilles

SORRY!

SO, THIS IS THE PAPER YOU WERE TALKING ABOUT?

I THINK THAT'S ABOUT MY MOM.

WHAT?

YEAH... SHE SAID SHE RAN AWAY.

SHE NEVER SAID ANYTHING GOOD ABOUT THE TOWN. SHE DIDN'T WANT TO GO BACK.

LIKE, *REALLY* DIDN'T WANT TO GO BACK. THINGS WERE STRAINED BETWEEN HER AND GRANDMA.

WHAT...

THE MEN HERE SNAP,
EVERY SINGLE ONE.

IS THAT...

OH GOD, AMY'S JAW?

YEAH, SHE AND HER MOM SURVIVED.

SORRY...

I'M NOT TALKING ABOUT THAT.

OKAY.

OH...GREAT, YOUR FRIENDS ARE LOOKING FOR YOU.

YEAH...
I INVITED
THEM.

WHAT?

I THOUGHT
THEY COULD
HELP.

MORE
IDEAS.

NO.

WHY
NOT?

YOU NEED TO GIVE PEOPLE A CHANCE.

I HAVE.

SORRY... SCARED HER OFF.

I KNEW SHE'D BAIL. AMANDA'S NOT NORMAL.

SO, WHAT WERE WE GOING TO TALK ABOUT?

LET ME TRY AND GRAB HER, OKAY?

AMANDA, PLEASE COME BACK.

I WON'T LET THEM BE JERKS.

TRUST ME.

DENIS!

CHRIS! QUIT DOING THAT.

I'M SORRY, SO SORRY, BUT WE NEED TO TALK.

CHRIS, IS EVERYTHING OKAY?

I DON'T KNOW... I JUST NEED TO TALK.

SOMEWHERE PRIVATE.

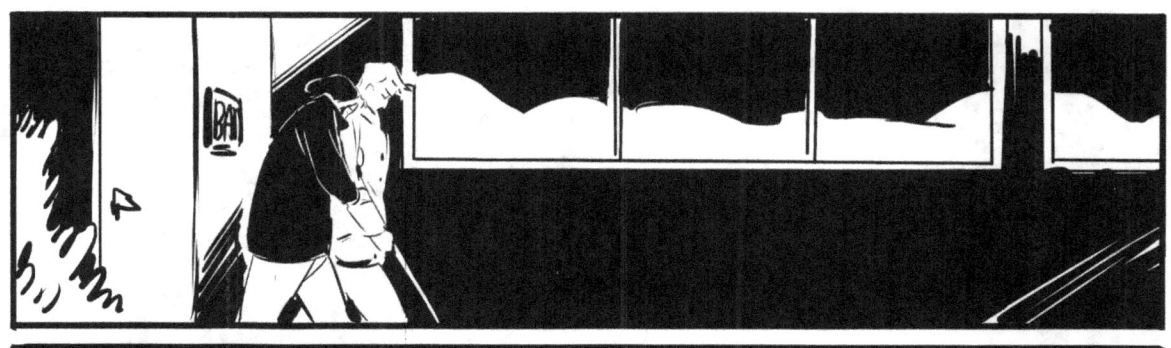

I HAVEN'T DONE ANYTHING. BUT SHE JUST WANTS TO SPEAK TO HER.

I DON'T KNOW WHAT SHE WANTS.

YOU KNOW I'M NOT LETTING HER NEAR MY DAUGHTER.

WHY DID YOU LET HER NEAR MY HOUSE THEN?

MARGIE SENT HER OUT,

I TRIED TO STOP HER.

THEY DIDN'T SPEAK, DID THEY?

SHE LET HER IN, BUT THAT'S IT. I THINK SHE GOT DISTRACTED BY FINCH.

GOOD... I GUESS.

I DON'T KNOW.

MAYBE IT WON'T BE THAT BAD?

YOU KNOW IT'S NEVER GOOD WITH THOSE MONSTERS.

YOU NEVER KNOW... SHE DOES LOVE TO TALK.

NO. I'M NOT DOING THIS.

I'M SORRY, DENIS. I'M SORRY, DON'T LEAVE ME, PLEASE.

I MEAN, I'M GOING TO TALK TO HER.

I WANT YOU TO TAKE ME THERE.

YOU CAN'T...

SHE'S DANGEROUS.

I DON'T CARE. TAKE ME TO MS. MAGPIE.

OH...
HELLO
AMANDA.

HUH?
YOU SURE
SOUND
EXCITED.

SORRY, I'M
JUST WORRYING
ABOUT YOUR
FATHER.

WHAT
HE DO?

HE'S
OUT LATE...

I WORRY.

HOW ARE YOU AND THE GILLES GIRL DOING?

THE TALK OF THE TOWN IS YOU'VE BECOME FAST FRIENDS.

OH STOP, I'M HAPPY FOR YOU. I KNEW YOU'D FIND A FRIEND.

SHE'S NOT MY FRIEND.

AMANDA...

MOM, I HAVE A QUESTION.

WHAT DO YOU KNOW ABOUT BERNADETTE GILLES?

I READ THAT SHE RAN AWAY YEARS AGO.

DENIS, ARE YOU SURE ABOUT THIS?

I'M NOT LETTING THIS GO ANY FURTHER.

BUT WHAT IF SHE KILLS YOU?

I DON'T WANT TO BE ALONE AGAIN.

ARE YOU TALKING TO MOTHER...?

HOW'D YOU MAKE IT GO AWAY?

EASY. MONSTERS DON'T HAVE HEARTS.

WITHOUT A HEART, THEY DON'T HAVE EMOTIONS OR DREAMS. THEY CAN'T DO ANYTHING.

THE STAR MONSTER BORROWED MY FRIEND'S HEART AND MS. MAGPIE IS BORROWING YOUR MOTHER'S....

BUT IF YOUR MOM TOLD THE MONSTER TO GO AWAY, WISHED FOR IT WITH ALL HER HEART...

I WAS GETTING TO IT.
WHEN I WAS WITH THE CONSUMPTION I DREAMED OF DESTROYING THE EARTH, BUT MY FATHER WOULDN'T LET ME.
WHEN I GREW UP, I MET A WITCH THAT DREAMED OF DESTROYING STARS.
AND THEY PUT THEM OUT ONE BY ONE.
You think that I...
could be great?

Bonus
Content

CHRIS, HOW DID YOU AND DENIS FIRST MEET?

I DIDN'T STALK HIM.

OH... OKAY? WHAT DO YOU LIKE MOST ABOUT DENIS?

WELL... UM... HE DOESN'T JUDGE ME...

AND HE'S SMART TOO. HE KNOWS SO MUCH ABOUT THE MONSTERS, AND EVEN WHEN I KNOW IT'S HOPELESS, HE MAKES ME FEEL LIKE THERE'S HOPE.

SO... WHEN'S THE WEDDING?

Wedding?
You're making
me blush.

DO YOU EVEN HAVE A FACE?

An expression.
I am the nothing,
I know not blushing brides
or the excitement of meeting mine.
I merely know that now the
borrowed desire I have is for
Amanda.
My Love.

COOL, HAVE FUN WITH THAT...
GIVE AMANDA A KISS FOR ME
WITH THAT FACE YOU DON'T HAVE.

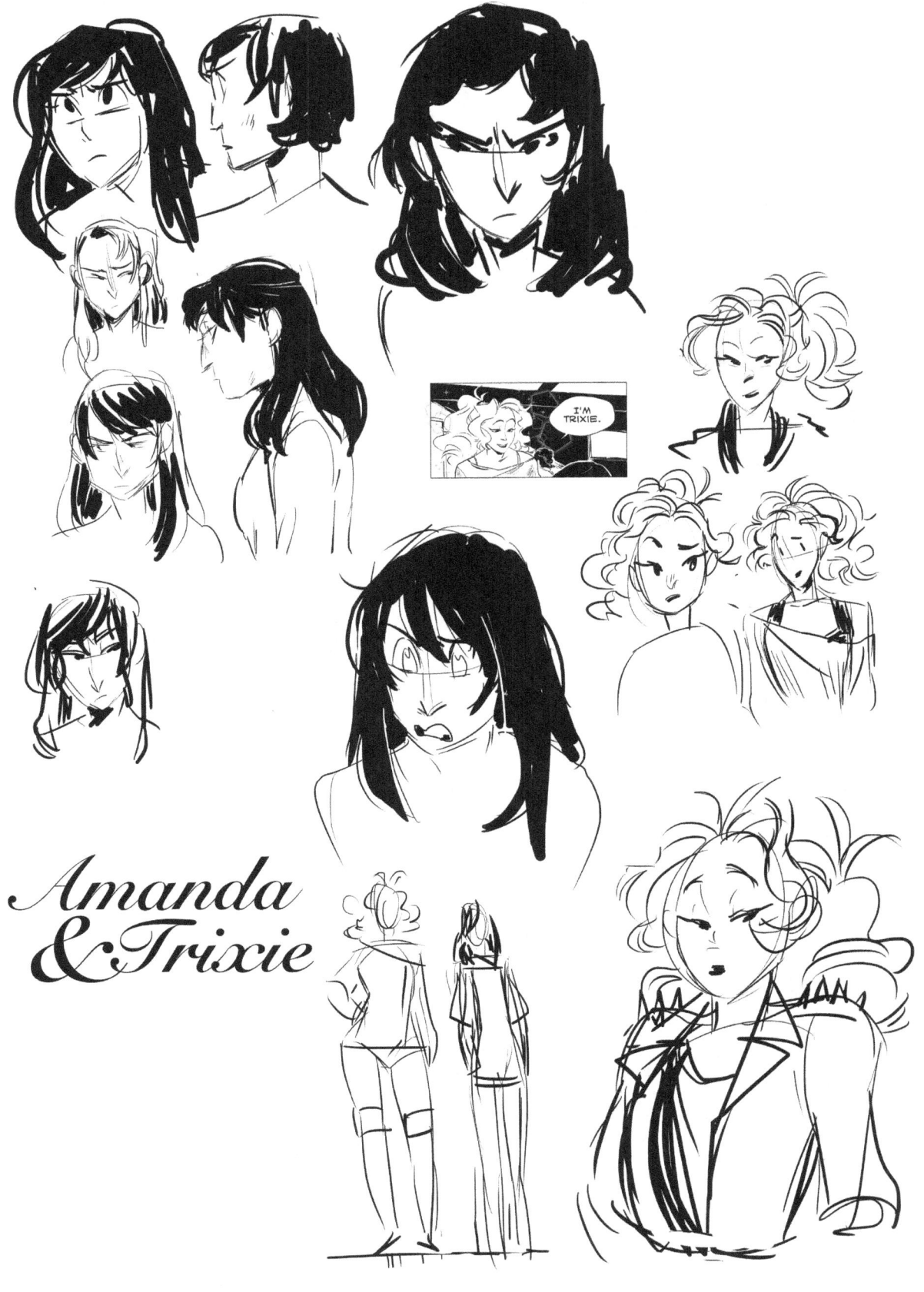

I'M TRIXIE.

Amanda & Trixie

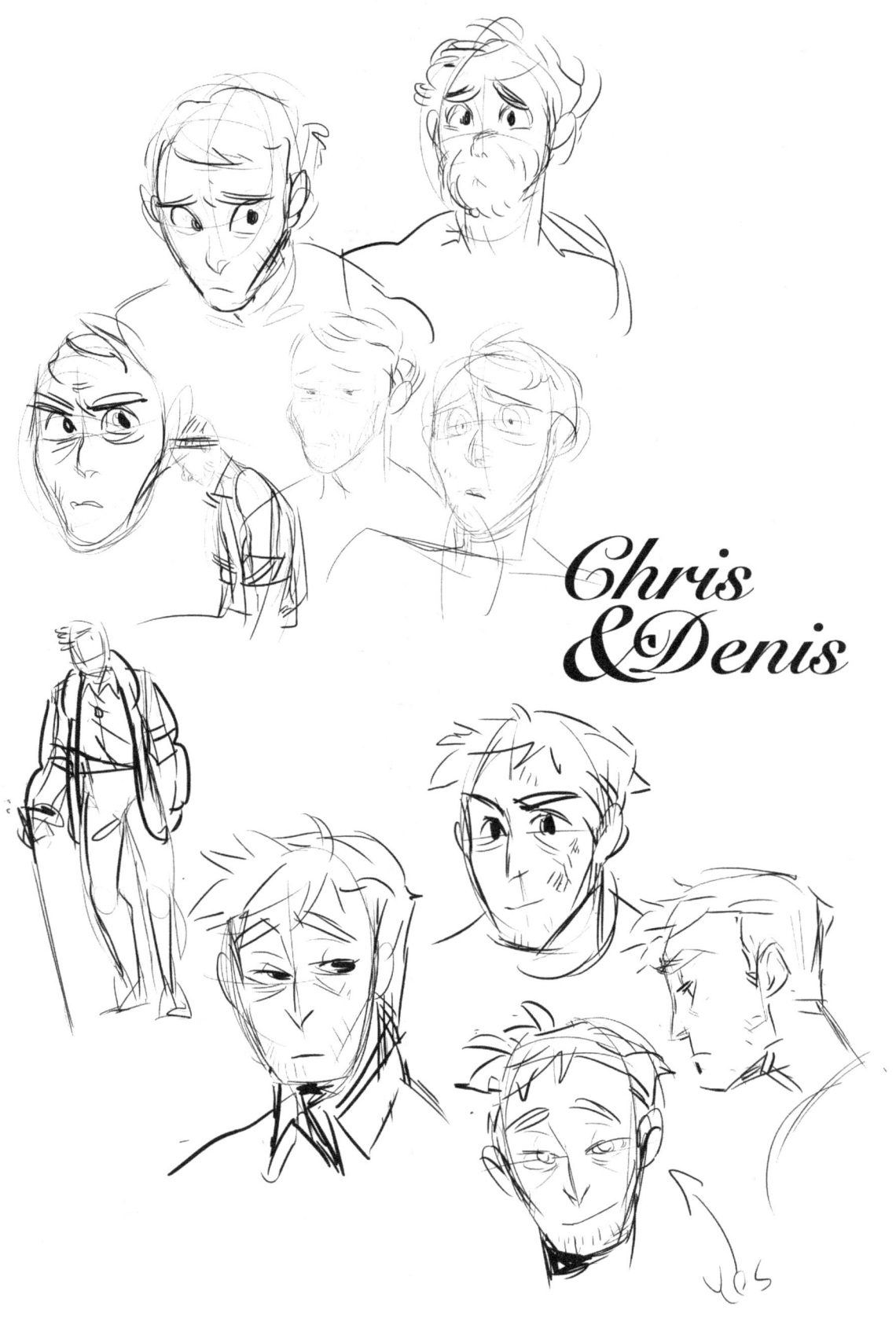

Chris
&Denis

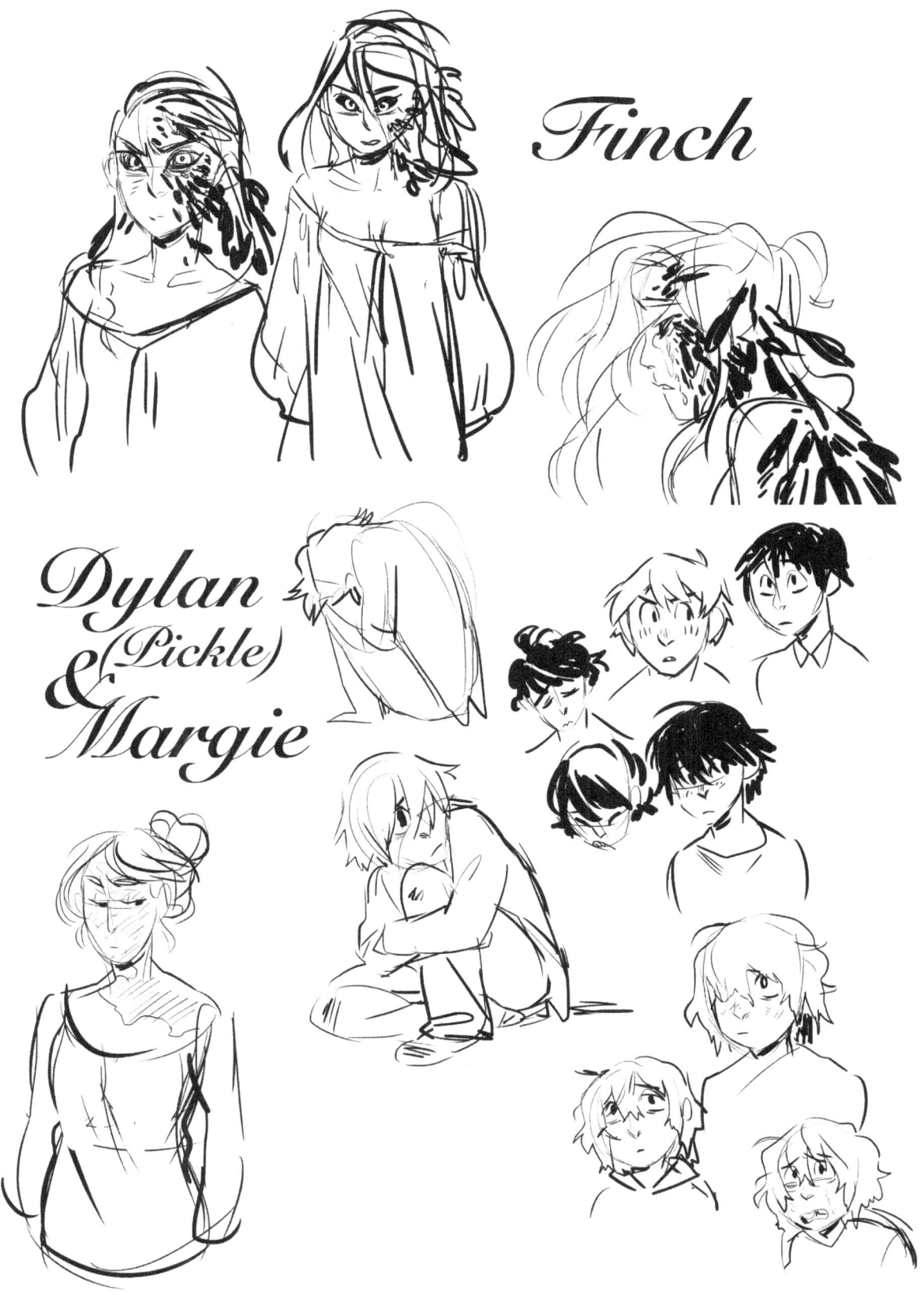

Finch

Dylan
(Pickle)
&
Margie

CONTINUE READING!
PRETTYMOUTHCOMIC.COM

www.ingramcontent.com/pod-product-compliance
Lightning Source LLC
Chambersburg PA
CBHW080824020726
47501CB00009B/2415